RAPTURED

RAPTURED

DEZNE FRASER

TATE PUBLISHING
AND ENTERPRISES, LLC

Published by Tate Publishing & Enterprises, LLC
127 E. Trade Center Terrace | Mustang, Oklahoma 73064 USA
1.888.361.9473 | www.tatepublishing.com

Tate Publishing is committed to excellence in the publishing industry. The company reflects the philosophy established by the founders, based on Psalm 68:11,
"The Lord gave the word and great was the company of those who published it."

Book design copyright © 2015 by Tate Publishing, LLC. All rights reserved.
Cover design by Maria Louella Mancao
Interior design by Honeylette Pino

Published in the United States of America

ISBN: 978-1-68118-609-2
1. Fiction / Romance / General
2. Fiction / Coming of Age
15.03.03

I would like to dedicate this book to all the young people in my generation. You all have impacted my life in so many ways.

ACKNOWLEDGMENT

I would like to acknowledge my family and loved ones who have been with me every step of the way, helped me, and supported me throughout all my years of life. To my family and loved ones, I thank you the for the love, care, contributions, and sacrifices that were made to make my life what it is today.

CONTENTS

INTRODUCTION

This is not just a story. It is the life of a young woman starting a new life. Her journey starts with changing transitions and opening new doors to opportunities in school, friends, family, new found bliss, and a transforming identity of her own image and self-concept. This woman's name is Elise Williams. Elise Williams is five foot six. She weighs 125 pounds. She is dark-skinned; the shape of her body is of an hourglass figure; her hair texture is soft, silky, and wavy; the width of her hair is thick and course; the length of her hair is short; and the color tone of her hair is pitch-black. Her eyes are oval-shaped, hazel, and medium-sized. Her face structure is square; eyebrows are slightly arched but bushy; nose shape highly crooked and bent to one side; and her lips are reddish pink, wide, and big.

Elise Williams's personality is known to be of a feminine and tomboy edge. She is known for being blunt, spontaneous, impulsive, intense, strong, independent, logical, determined, magnetic, mysterious, objective, and passionate. Her career pursuits are to become a CSI detective and a journalist. Her favorite hobbies are acting, playing the piano, and talking on the phone with her best friend. She likes to wear warm, sporty clothing that gives her comfort, flexibility, versatility, and laid-back style. The clothes that she wears that describe her style are: bulky yet colorful sweaters, thick-collared turtlenecks, long-sleeved shirts, zipped hoodies, denim jeans, sweatpants, and regular pants. Her tone of voice when speaking is loud, outspoken, abrasive, sarcastic, and sometimes high-pitched.

Elise Williams's role is the protagonist—the main character in this story. As you will come to know, this woman discovers through her journey that life comes with its own challenges, emotional disturbance, and trying difficulties. In those times of struggle, she found peace, joy, laughter, and happiness. One element in her journey was apparently missing in her life; it's the one thing that she was afraid to face—the popular four-letter word called *love*.

She comes to see that love is a battlefield that cannot be won unless you are willing to fight. As her journey continues, she soon realizes that love begins with loving yourself, others, and God before loving a significant bachelor.

This young bachelor whom she comes across in her journey is named Stephan Banks. Stephan Banks is six foot one and weighs 180 pounds. The figure of his body is healthy and skinny. His hair texture is smooth, and the appearance of the facial hair is shaved, but not removed. Skin complexion is light-caramel brown. Eyes are somewhat wide, circular, and dark brown. Eyebrows are untrimmed, but still have a curved shape to them. Nose is short and it looks airbrushed and perky. Lips are golden brown, but have a rosy-pink hue of color to them; the lips are perfectly full and lumpy and the lip size is medium. The structure of the face is oval-shaped and his ears are correctly pinned back together in one place.

Stephan Banks's personality is one of intrigue and unpredictability. He is thought of as being intuitive, calm, quiet, reflective, raspy, confident, smooth, non-judgmental, thoughtful, respectful, affectionate, and caring. His career attributes is to pursue fashion design and runway modeling and eventually soon after, became an actor. His favorite hobbies are yoga, soccer, cooking, and going to VIP parties. Stephan's role is the protagonist's helper by being Elise's guardian, advisor, and friend.

In this story, Elise Williams will come to know a couple of friends who guide her through her ongoing journey. Elise's close friend Matthew is the person in her life who was there when she needed someone to talk to about almost anything in particular except secular music. Matthew is five foot seven and weighs 175 pounds. His body appearance is skinny, slightly tall, and average. His skin color is dark-skinned and his eye color is dark brown; hair is shaved and cut. His personality is wholesome, conservative, modest, and humorous. His known occupation is public health services. His hobbies are soccer, reading, and studying.

Amy, Elise's best buddy whom she came close to know on a daily basis, is known as her example of how to be pure, holy, and righteous in the eyes of God and her prototype of traumatizing experiences that she, Elise, could go through but has not gone through in her life. Amy is Elise's life-learning lesson. She is five foot tall and weighs 133 pounds. Her body appearance is slim and petite. Her skin color is coco brown and eye color is dark brown. Hair is frizzy and curly. Her personality is sweet, kind, helpful, loving, and sincere. Her current occupation is in the field of writing and research consulting. She likes movies, art, drawing, and decorating.

Lisa is Elise's friend whom she came to know a little of but has come to know after a few conversations and school hangouts. She is the kind of friend whom Elise can spill out gossip of celebrities, boys, and whatever appears to be juicy talk and laughter. Her height is five foot eight and her body weight is 135 pounds. Her body appearance is of an hourglass figure, pretty tall, normal. Skin color is olive complexion and her eye color is dark brown. Hair is wavy, dark brown, soft, silky, and long. Her personality is crazy, funny, sarcastic, direct, and hardworking. Her occupation is in the field of world studies and communications. Her hobbies include playing rugby, listening to music, and hanging out with friends.

Denise is Elise's friend whom she met during the first few days at school. Denise showed Elise around the school and told her about the clubs and activities at Tampa State University and what she does for fun. Denise's height is five foot four. Her weight is 129 pounds. Her body appearance is slim, average, petite, and short. Her skin color is that of an olive light complexion that is clear of blemishes and dark spots. Her eye color is dark brown and her hair color is dark, silky, and medium cut. Her personality is witty, smart, chatty, sociable, and outgoing. Her occupation involves dancing, music, food, and culture. Her hobbies are partying, clubbing, drinking, smoking, and celebrating life.

Jose is Elise's friend who came into her life when she was new to the school and has welcomed her to the social environment of Tampa State University. Jose's height is five foot six. His weight is 136 pounds. Jose's body appearance is short, fat, and average. Jose's skin color is that of an olive complexion that is tender, supple, and soft. His eye color is dark brown and hair is spiky, and dark black. Jose's personality is cool, relaxed, and laid-back. Jose's current occupation is him being a student and a working employee. His hobbies are learning about culture, going to social gatherings, and having fun.

Scarlett is Elise's long-time friend who knows or has known Elise for years. Elise can come to Scarlett and talk about anything and everything under the sun with no limits. Elise finds freedom and liberty in her friendship with Scarlett. Scarlett's height is five foot six. Her body appearance is slightly tall, hourglass figure, and thick-skinned. Her skin color is that of a dark brown complexion that is smooth and soft. Scarlett's weight is 140 pounds. Her eye color is dark brown, and her hair is dark, short, and curly. Scarlett's personality is silly, goofy, imaginative, blunt, adventurous, spontaneous, impulsive, and caring. Her hobbies are reading, writing, playing guitar, knitting, listening to music, and counseling others. Scarlett's current occupations are being an author, life coach, and language translator.

Felicia is Elise's friend who provides Elise a fresh perspective on how to approach people in dealing with friendships that need rebuilding and provides guidance on how to conduct oneself as a lady when it comes to guys and Elise's wanted bachelor that all the young ladies go after. Felicia is 140 pounds. Her height is five foot six. Her body appearance is nicely curved, and has an hourglass frame to her figure. The color of her eyes is dark brown. Her skin is dark and smooth. Her hair is thick, wavy, and black. Her personality is spiky, sarcastic, humorous, mature, and kind. Her hobbies are watching movies, video recording, taking pictures, chatting, cooking, dancing, eating, and learning.

Her current occupation is being a studious student at Tampa State University.

Monica is Elise's friend whom she met at Tampa State University through Amy who has known Monica for awhile. Monica is the kind of friend who finds every opportunity to talk to Elise when time is convenient for both of them to socialize and catch up on what's going on around the Tampa State University campus. Monica is 128 pounds. Her height is five foot five. Her body appearance is that of an average thickness in curves and shape. Her skin complexion is dark brown and soft. Her eye color is dark brown, and her hair color is dark and curly. Her personality is unyielding, strong-minded, receptive, and thoughtful. Her hobbies are dancing, singing, reading, exercising, instant messaging, talking on the phone, and general fun where the party is. Monica's current occupation is being an office assistant and student at Tampa State University.

Eunice is Elise's friend who is known for being a profound and serious leader in her life to guide her and redirect her focus toward God at all times even if she does not like the way he imposes his opinions. Eunice is also a close confidant for Stephan and are like brothers toward one another in everything they say and do; Eunice is the "other half" of Stephan's behavior and personality. Eunice and Stephan cannot separate themselves from each other. They are like "peas in a pod." Elise met Eunice while attending a Bible club at Tampa State University. Eunice is

130 pounds. His height is five foot six. His body appearance is of a lanky, slightly tall, and skinny stature. Eunice's skin color is dark. His hair is trimmed sharply and is lightly thin. His eyes are dark brown and round. His personality is somewhat eccentric and awkward at times when the moments are inappropriate, but he is also a serious, ambitious, and hardworking individual unlike his "other half" who appears to be uncertain about his ambitions and being unpredictable. His hobbies are reading the Bible daily, evangelizing, preaching, teaching, and proclaiming the Good News of the Gospel to all people. His current occupation is being a student at Tampa State University and establishing a career in business.

Peter is Elise's friend that she slowly came to know after a few friendly exchanges and Bible club appearances at Tampa State University. Peter is a part of Elise's life; he provides her spiritual inspiration, peace, transparency, tranquility, and harmony. Peter is 130 pounds. His height is five foot seven. Peter's body appearance is short, average, and normal. His skin color is dark brown and has a coco brazen texture. His hair is nicely shaved, round, and carefully brushed. His eye color is dark and oval-shaped. His personality is quiet, humble, obedient, God-fearing, studious, unyielding, and determined. His hobbies are reading the Bible, studying, praying, fellowshipping, and enjoying the company of others. His current occupation is being a student at Tampa State University and being an employee.

Chris is Elise's friend whom she met the first time she went to the Bible club at Tampa State University. Chris provides happiness and joy in Elise's life when things are a bit shaky and out of place for her to deal with. Chris is a close companion in Stephan's life. Chris knows Stephan more than anyone else can count and tells Stephan everything that is on his mind. He and Stephan are like brothers to each other; they go and do everything together. Chris is 132 pounds. His height is five foot seven. His body appearance is average, short, and muscular somewhat. His eyes are oval and have a light brown color to them. His skin complexion is a sunny bronze texture that is soft and transparent. His hair is dark and nicely shaped to perfection. Chris has a personality that is sweet, tender-harden, calm, relaxed, and nonabrasive. His hobbies are praying, worshipping the Lord, singing, and hanging out with Stephan. His current occupation is anonymous at the time.

Sean is Elise's friend whom she met the first time in acting/theater class at Tampa State University. Sean provides assistance and encouragement throughout the school semester and was always courteous and respectful toward Elise, like a gentleman. Sean was the enlightenment and humor in Elise's life when things were sour and messy. Sean is 136 pounds. His height is five foot ten. His body appearance is average, short, and muscular in some areas of his body. His eyes are medium-sized and dark brown. His skin complexion is dark-skinned, soft, and tender. His hair is densely shaved and dark. His personality is humorous, sarcastic, gentlemanly, kind, charming, and outspoken. His hobbies are riding motorcycles, partying, working, and hanging leisurely with his buddies. His current occupation is in a financial agency.

Vince is six foot one. His weight is 140 pounds. His height is slightly tall. His body is muscular and macho. Vince's hair is dark; it appears shaggy and disoriented. His skin complexion is dark-skinned and soft. Eyes are wide and circular. The eye color is dark brown. Vince's personality is vindictive, instigative, schemeful, intellectually savvy, convincing, and reckless. Vince is the antagonist in this story. He views Stephan as his opposite and an enemy or threat to his well-being and integrity. His hobbies are writing, reading, and instant messaging. He parties hard. His current occupation is unknown.

Elise wants to find love and is too apprehensive to try. In the end, will she chase after love when love has chased after her or will she miss a divine love of providence that God has presented before her? As you will see, her journey still continues and has not stopped. She still has a lot to discover as she walks through the road of her life just like you will.

1

NEW BEGINNINGS

Elise's first day begins with her waking up from her puffed-up bed with pillows to the bed rest layered across the bed. She walks to her narrow bathroom and begins to brush her stained white teeth repeatedly for five minutes until she is satisfied with her white smile. She goes on to wash her crusty face and once done, go to the white oval-shaped bathtub to cleanse her body with fragrant soaps and scrubs. Fifteen minutes into the hot boiled stream of water, she exits gradually out the tub, wraps her body with the warm comfort of a cotton towel, and walks out of the bathroom to her room to style herself with clothing and jewelry.

Once dressed fully, she urgently looks over at her cell phone to check the time. She then quickly exits her room and walks down the steps toward the living room. She grabs her backpack, cell phone, jacket, and runs outside to catch her taxicab and heads off hastily to Tampa State University not too far from where she lives. Elise Williams lives in Tampa, Florida, with her fifty-year-old mother and eighteen-year-old sister. Elise Williams is a junior undergraduate at Tampa State University. She is studying to become a CSI detective and journalist.

Elise Williams now arrives at Tampa State University. She quickly pays the taxi driver twenty-five dollars for her hastily trip to college. She grabs her backpack, wraps it around her neck, shoulders, and she exits the noisy gas-guzzler taxicab. Elise walks peacefully toward the two glass doors of the entrance of Tampa State University. She walks through the doors with full anticipation of a new crisp beginning of a new school year. Elise Williams walks along the wide open space of the hallway that is filled with flags hung high on each side of the ceiling, white fresh walls of the school's poster on each corner she passed, marble-glazed tile floors, tall poles attached to the ceiling that resembled a Roman Catholic embassy, large school centers, and a population of multicultural nationalities. Elise instinctively thought to herself that she was finally home and where she wanted to be. Elise was ready for a new chapter in her life—new college, new friends, new teachers, new curriculum, and a new major career change. Upon that change, Elise had to adjust her ways of handling schedules, transportation trips, and getting acquainted with her new school location. With enthusiasm and eagerness in Elise's ambitious drive, Elise took it upon herself to ask students around the Tampa State University as well as security guards where she could register for her three challenging classes. One being chemistry, the others being biology and a journalism class.

Elise wanders aimlessly on the sidewalk peaceful and rushes to find where the student admissions office is. She approaches a crowd and asks, "Excuse me, do anyone of you know where the student admissions office is located?" Several of them come near Elise while in the middle of a crowded campus area, where tables all covered with decorated soft cloths with the school's initial and a display of school products which students are selling or fundraising. Some of the students nod and extend their arms to point to where they think the office is. Viewing their body languages, Elise seems a little not convinced of their replies to her urgent question. So to avoid the total embarrassment of being seen as a "nobody" who knows nothing about this town and school she will be attending, Elise takes up the courage to ask a prominent authority figure, but as soon as she wanders to find one, a well-mannered female security guard walks closely by her and courteously asks, "Do you need help?"

Elise impulsively states her need for urgency in her time of overwhelming thoughts and feelings of this new experience and says, "Yes, can you help me find where I can register for classes?"

The female security guard then says in a nice comfortable tone, "Sure."

While the security guard is by Elise's left side, Elise slows down her pace to follow the security guard's lead to the glass entrance door of the student admission center that signs in print, "Student Admissions Office: Enter and go straight to the admissions desk." The female security guard gently opens the door with her left hand while Elise takes her time walking up the pavement from the sidewalk to go to the door of the student admissions office. Elise scrolled in through the door while the security guard has the door extended open. Elise calmly walks in the student admissions office and notices a load of students lining up (one student behind another) to register for classes, financial aid, photo identification, class drops, and filling out forms and applications to be registered to the school. Other students on the one hand are cutting to the chase of waiting in long, exhausting lines by registering for classes on the computer through the school's website. Several others are chatting upon themselves loudly not having a care in the world what is happening around them and some students are just lethargic in their "roll-around" chairs looking around the office oblivious in what to do next as a student task in preparing for the school semester. While in the school office, Elise hears a staff announcing to everyone who needs to get a picture taken for a new school ID to get in line. Before Elise walks leisurely in line to get a picture taken, she walks quickly to the register's desk to speak to one of the admissions counselors about a major and the classes she wants to take.

Elise proclaims soundly, "I would like to find out how I can apply for a major and register for my classes."

The admissions counselor simply tells Elise, "Here is a Tampa State University catalog with a list of the current majors you can choose from. Fill out this registration form by placing your major in the blank slot along with listing your classes that you would want to register for and then come back to the admissions desk and have your classes paid for with credit or cash online on one of the available computers right behind you or you can pay immediately in person after you register."

Elise, seeming decisive, makes her decision and states, "I think I'll register and pay for my classes right after in person."

In the process of paying for her classes, Elise's cell phone kept ringing continuously nonstop inside her bag. Elise ignored the nagging vibration of such a small technical device and continued to complete her other obligations in the student admissions office. Elise went on urgently to wait in line to get her photograph taken for student identification.

Students in front of Elise appeared to be straining their legs while standing to wait for their turns. After five minutes, the line went faster as Elise waited patiently to have a seat in the photo chair. Elise was behind one student whose photo was about to be taken. The student walked close to the chair, sat down, and was told what body positions to maneuver when being faced in front of the photographer. The student posed very happily with a grin on the face as the camera flashed. The student soon stood upright and walked toward the exit of the student admissions office. Elise now came forth with readiness to have a snap of her photo taken. Elise stood standing confidently as the photographer said to her in a giddy voice, "Are you ready for a photo to be taken of you for your new student ID?"

Elise, still standing with a smile on her face, says cheerfully, "Yes, I am ready."

Elise moves close to the photo chair, turns her body around to have the chair right behind to support her when she bends her legs, hips, and back to comfortably sit in the plastic aluminum photo chair. The photographer grabs the professional digital camera and uses his finger to snap a photo. While holding the digital camera tightly with both hands, the photographer says, "Look into the camera and smile."

Elise smiles with an open grin of white clean teeth. The photographer shows her the first slide of the sample photo inserted inside the frame of a labeled and printed font of the Tampa State University ID that is colored red and black around the inserted student photograph. When the photographer shows Elise her first slide of her photograph, she twists her face in dislike and says promptly to the photographer, "Ugh...this photo looks really bad. Can I take another photograph?"

The photographer responds, "Sure, let's try again."

Elise in agreement says, "Okay."

Elise sits in the photo chair with her back extended up, chest high, and head held high and grins with the same fixed smile when facing the digital camera. The camera flashes rapidly as Elise smiles, then Elise rises up comfortably from the plastic photo chair. She sees her new photograph that the photographer has in his hand. The photographer hands her the cheery photograph and Elise walks out from all the busyness and finds her way to the exit of the student admissions office. As Elise walks through the crowd of people outside on a bright sunny day, her cellular phone rings inside her bag. She searches through her bag and latches her hand onto the cell phone and places it by her car. Elise says, "Hello?"

The caller replies, "Hello."

Elise slowly recognizes the familiar voice on the line. "Hello, Mom, everything went just fine. I selected a major and registered for the classes I needed to take."

"That is very good, so you are thinking of purchasing books?"

"Yes, I will purchase the books for my classes online at home."

"Okay, that is good, talk to you later."

"Talk to you later too, Mom. Love you." Elise ends the conversation by hanging up her cell phone.

Elise continues to walk among the crowds of people and spots a bench that she could sit upon to rest her legs while she waits patiently for a taxicab to take her home. Over the weekend, Elise relaxes at home by talking to her best friend Scarlett about her new transition from a boring and strict university board school to a more diversified and social atmosphere of livelihood and opportunity at Tampa State University. Elise says excitingly on the phone with Scarlett, "I am looking forward to a brand new school. I have been locked up in the house for five straight years with just me and the computer as my companion taking online classes and being engrossed in the books with completely no social interaction with outside world." Elise continues on her topic by emphasizing her lack of social interaction by quickly stating to Scarlett on the phone, "Really, the only time I had some social interaction was when I took a class one semester at my board school where the teacher was by the chalkboard and I was sitting in the back row inconspicuous and scared to flinch my body while being surrounded by so many students in the classroom."

Scarlett responds in understanding by stating, "Oh, I am so glad you will be going to Tampa State University. You will really like it." Scarlett continues to explain what Tampa State University is like in her own words. "With Tampa State University, the classes are affordable, the teachers are willing to help you, and you will easily make good friends. Trust me, Elise, you will really like Tampa State University. Give it a try and you will see."

Elise begins on a fresh start in her life, school, and social environment. She does not know what to expect or what will come of the day, but she knows it will be good. Elise spurts up gradually from her cozy white puffy pillows and white linen bedsheets and walks to the bathroom; she softly cleanses her dirty, itchy face with a face mask and uses lukewarm temperature water; she pats her face with a soft cotton face cloth. She then grabs a tube of Colgate toothpaste, squirts it horizontally across the toothbrush base, holds the toothbrush in her right hand, and brushes her teeth for five minutes.

With the toothpaste foam in her mouth, Elise turns the sink faucet on cold, and with the water on, uses both of her cold hands to sporadically rinse her mouth out of the white foam. She then goes by the white deep bathtub, turns the tub faucet on in clockwork motion to warm the temperature of the water up. She dips herself slowly in the steamy water and baths herself softly for fifteen minutes. After fifteen minutes of bathing, she lifts herself up with her fully lush body in wet particles on the skin out of the deep wide bathtub. She goes to grab her tender white robe, puts it through her fingers onto her arms, and covers up the rest of her lower body parts with the robe. With her skin dry, she applies body butter coco butter from head to toe in slow motion and begins to place layers of clothing on her supple, glazed brown bronze, coco skin. She then puts on her Skechers brand sneakers on her feet with socks on, plumps up her white puffy pillow cases and pillows, neatly irons her bedsheets, and folds and flattens the bedsheets in place; she takes her cotton polyester blanket and covers up her entire bed.

Since Elise's hair already has braid extensions, she does not have to worry about styling her hair in any fashion or form, she just goes ahead and puts foundation, concealer, bronzer, eye shadow, eye liner, and lipstick on to beautify the face, but she chooses not to go that direction and simply just decides to have a face of "Miss Plain Jane." Elise walks quickly down the steps and walks toward the living room to exit the front door and catches her taxicab to head off to Tampa State University. She arrives at Tampa State University twenty-five minutes early before her 9:45 a.m. journalism class. She glances aimlessly and observes without acknowledgement of what is happening at her present moment in time. She soon realizes as she watches the clock tick from 9:30 a.m. to 9:37 a.m. that she now is in a school with no virtual walls and technology at her fingertips. Elise is at a school with real people and real physical interaction that appears to spring about direct and indirect communication with staff, workers, teachers, and students. The clock goes gradually to 9:40 a.m. while Elise is sitting down causally in a hard rubber chair surrounded by other isolated chairs with no person to fill them in and an empty clear, round table. Elise feels a certain jolt in her body as her wrist starts to reflex and turn adjacent for her eyes to look at her white circular watch. Urgently, she gets up hastily from the chair she was sitting in, and spurts to the building site of where her journalism class would be. Elise is in the human communication building, she asks random people in the building, "Where can I find the Introduction to Journalism class?" A woman in her mid-forties with dark brown hair, olive skin complexion that appears to be slightly wrinkled, and has eyes that are round, dark, and deep. Body figure seems lanky, but normal; and her demeanor is astute; this woman comes upfront directly toward Elise and answers her wavering question, "Yes, madam, you are looking for the journalism class, right?"

Elise follows with a fast reply, "Yes."

Elise and this woman are standing five feet from each other as they are talking face-to-face. The woman walks with Elise as they are having informal conversation while in the human communications building. As they walk past each classroom on the left window view, the woman says to Elise, "Here we are. Room HC 205 on your right corner."

As the woman is making her statement, she signals to Elise with her right finger, pointing to where the journalism would be. Elise moves to her right side to walk near to where the classroom is located, when the woman says directly, "Well, it was nice meeting you. Hope to catch up with you again."

Elise quickly turns her head towards the woman and says gladly, "Thank you so much for helping me out. Hope to see you around."

Elise went to her classroom on the right-hand corner and the woman went to the other side of the human communication building and did her duties and current obligations. One interesting factor though, Elise and the woman did not mention their names to each other. It was just a rare occurrence. Now Elise walks by the window of her journalism class. She nosily peeks in the glass and sees a row of focused and attentive students pinned at the teacher's attention (at least the majority of them are concentrated on the teacher's attention from Elise's view of sight); the rest of the students may be looking at each other in small groups, moving the mouths in small closed-in conversation. A few maybe sloughing in their desk chairs having a lazy posture as if they are about to snore softly, some put their head flat on their desk to fall asleep in class as the teacher is lecturing. Elise grabs a hold of the metal crease door knob, turns it slowly; while trying to not allow a creaking effect penetrate into the classroom to let others know that "someone new" has just arrived at the scene. As she turns the door knob, the door clicks and she presses against the door as it opens for her to come inside and find a seat. Elise scans to find herself a seat. She gradually walks toward the middle aisle and shyly moves unobstructively to not offend anyone by her physical presence. When she saw an empty seat in the front right by the middle aisle, she quickly arranged her school bag and jacket, and sat comfortably in the desk chair with her legs extended out in a relaxed position with notebook, folders, and textbook at hand to her side.

Posture and body composure are centered and cognitive attention are "fixed" on the teacher while blocking out noises from the students. The teacher asked those that just came into class late to introduce themselves in cordial respect. Elise slowly raised herself from her seat and said nervously to Professor Thompson, "Uh, hello, Professor, I am a new student at Tampa State University that just entered into this journalism class."

The professor looked at Elise unsure of what she was saying and looked at her class student roster to look for Elise's name on the list. Professor Thompson said to Elise urgently, "What is your name again, because I don't see your name on the class roster."

Elise said hastily to the professor, "My name is Elise Williams." Elise said all her statements to Professor Thompson all while she was up from her seat standing while holding the table desk.

Professor Thompson told Elise in a stern tone in front of the classmates, "Since I do not see your name on my class roster, and you said that you signed up for this journalism class, you need to check with the register and admissions office that you registered for this class."

Elise says sheepishly to the professor, "Okay" and slides back into her seat slowly.

Professor Thompson thoroughly explains the rules and guidelines that are expected of the classroom. The students look at her in mockery and ridicule by not taking her words seriously. The professor gives all the students, including Elise, warnings for failing the class procedures and not passing the class with an acceptable grade. The professor states sternly to the class the class work expectations and what she requires from every student and goes over the daily routines and tasks given to the students to complete in fourteen weeks as part of the journalism course. As a good student as Elise was, she went home every week to complete her homework assignments, participated in classroom discussions, and completed assigned projects all on time for every weekly class session until the class course was over. While in the midst of being in the journalism class, Elise met someone new that was young as she was or maybe a bit younger than she was. This new person's name was Mary. Several weeks into class, Elise sat in the front row of the classroom near Professor Thompson and saw

Mary appear near Elise and noticed the seat was empty, so Mary said kindly to Elise, "Is anyone sitting here?"

Elise replied kindly, "No."

Mary looks at Elise innocently in the eye and says sweetly in tone, "Can I sit by here?"

Elise looks Mary nicely in the eyes nicely to her. "Sure!"

Mary sits in her chair and says to Elise nicely with a smile even though she appears to be scared to talk to Elise but urges to speak and introduces herself by saying, "Hi, how are you? My name is Mary."

"Hi, nice to meet you, my name is Elise."

"Nice to meet you too."

A few classes later into the journalism class, Mary continues to sit by Elise and becomes friendly toward her. She offers Elise a little folded flyer of a nonprofit organization formulated into a Bible group club and explains what the club is about.

Elise responsively asks, "When does the bible group club start and when can I go?"

"The club starts Mondays and Wednesdays from 2:00 p.m. to 5:00 p.m. every week, and you should come."

Elise, without a decision, says in agreement, "Okay, I'll see."

Elise takes the flyer from Mary and puts it in her purse pocket and when class is over; Elise says a kind good-bye to Mary as Mary smiles back. With the school semester still new and fresh in Elise's mind, she meets and greets people she sees in school but continues to have her focus on her studies and completes her school work at home. With the weeks and months gone by, Elise stayed steady on her course work and attended her classes like a good student. While attending school, Elise was finishing up on a biochemistry course project with her group classmates. Forty-five minutes later, Elise completed her project and submitted her portion of the project to her biology teacher, Mr. Nelson. Her class finished around 2:00 p.m. and Elise decided to go outside in the sun and wait for her taxicab ride. Elise was sitting on the cement bench that was adjacent from the campus student center of Tampa State University. While Elise was sitting on the cement bench with the sun shining around her presence, she felt the wind sway amongst her mist and was observing the weather around her. While continuing to observe the weather, Elise heard five people talking loudly amongst themselves in a heated debate. Out of the five people, two of them were non-Christian believers; the others were professed Christians as it seems to their declaration of "Christian banners," the three individuals were of two young females and one young man. The two young females were standing in conjunction with the young man as part of their community defense of support. However, the young man was arguing with one of the two men that were non-Christians. The young man declaring in his debate to the non-Christian believer that Jesus Christ is the Way, the Truth, and the Life and should not be taken into mockery. The nonbeliever refused to accept what the young Christian man was saying about Christ and was not willing to believe what the truth was and literally "slapped" the young Christian man in the face by accusing him of blasphemy. After accusing the young Christian man of lies, the young man and his female companions departed in their argument debate and the non-Christian man left with his male friend. As Elise was watching the individuals depart in their separate ways, Elise noticed the two female ladies and the young man come in her direction. As they were coming toward Elise as she was sitting by herself, she quickly said, "Hey, I noticed that you all were having a heated conversation over there, what were you all talking about and doing?"

One of the ladies facing Elise said, "Well, me and my friends Matthew and Lisa were just over there trying to tell others around campus about Jesus and to get them to join our Bible group club at Tampa State University."

Elise, seeming eager and curious to get information from them, asked them, "Oh, wow, can you tell me more?"

The young lady said excitedly, "Yeah, sure!"

The other young lady said, "Our Bible group has bible study, worship, prayer, and fellowship. Also, the club begins every Monday and Wednesday from 2:00 to 5:00 p.m. Everyone is welcome to come." Then the young lady asks, "Do you believe in Christ and who is Christ to you?"

Elise says to the young lady with Lisa and Matthew by her side, "I believe in Jesus Christ and stand firm that to know Jesus you must believe for yourself because a lot of Christians claim that they know Jesus and are Christian, but don't live up to their Christian walk with the Lord and go back to their 'old man way' of sinning in the world."

The young lady, Lisa, and Matthew were flabbergasted and amazed by Elise's spoken word of intellect. Their amazement showed in their faces; the young lady said to Elise in curiosity of her name, "What is your name?"

Elise replied, "My name is Elise."

Melissa is the sister of Lisa. Lisa stated her name to Elise. Matthew stated his name to Elise. Elise asked each person's name in curiosity, "What is each of your names?"

The young lady said to Elise, "My name is Melissa."

Melissa asked Elise for her e-mail. "What is your e-mail?"

Elise replied promptly, "My e-mail is EliseJ.W@aol.com."

Melissa said to Elise as Lisa and Matthew were looking at her, "EliseJ.W@aol.com?"

Elise, in agreement to Melissa, said, "Yes." Elise, eagerly convinced by the invitation, thought about what the three individuals have said to her and tells them, "Sounds like something I might like. I will think about coming and consider this great offer. Thanks so much!"

The young lady Melissa and her sister Lisa, and the young man Matthew depart by saying to Elise in a greeting, "We'll see you around."

Elise says cheerfully to all of them, "See you around."

2

FIRST SIGHT

Elise returns to school to continue her studies. Before her classes start, Elise grabs breakfast from the ten-dollar menu. Elise selects her choice of eggs, bacon, sausage, hash browns, and a carton of orange juice. Elise gets into a line of students waiting to pay for her breakfast. Elise goes forth and pays the cashier the items that she put in place of the cashier counter.

Elise exits the food cafe with her breakfast and finds a seat in the cafeteria overlooking the mass of students chatting, socializing; some are standing and roaming around the cafeteria, and some are heading out of the cafeteria to enter the buildings of the Tampa State University campus center. While Elise eats her breakfast, she observes and watches the crowd of students enjoying themselves in laughter and amusement and takes out her iPod out of her backpack, plugs her headphones on her ears, and listens to a genre of music.

Elise then goes to class for journalism, participates in class activities, writes notes, communicates with the class group and instructor, then heads off to her chemistry class to complete a few hands-on assignments demonstrated throughout the class, and is given lab assignments to do for homework. After Elise is done with what she has to do for each of her classes, Elise becomes desperately hungry, searches for the elevator, tip-toes toward the elevator entrance, clicks with her finger to press the lightened elevator button, watches above as the lighted flashy numbers appear, 3…2…1, and instantly, the elevator opens up for Elise to go right inside. The elevator door closes shut; Elise remains stationed in until she watches the flashing lights go by. Elise hears a "ting" sound; the elevator door opens and she exits out on the first floor to go toward the food cafe. Elise finds a table to place her bag and marks it as her territory so that no one would take her seat. Elise looks through the cafeteria aisle with the intention of grabbing on to the cheapest and least expensive meal she could find.

The least expensive food to fit her appetite was pizza—pizza with the price of $2.25 for added topping on each pizza slice; $1.00 added to the lunch meal for purchase of a soda, such as Dr. Pepper to fit Elise's delight. Elise then begins to have a high sweet tooth, and with the pleasure in mind, snatches on the side, a velvety fudge chocolate cake all sealed and ready for her to gauge down and eat to her heart's desire. Elise once again waits for her turn in line to pay for her pizza, Dr. Pepper, and chocolate cake.

When the next person goes ahead with the purchase of his or her food, Elise comes next in line to purchase her delicious food. Elise purchases her food and exits the food cafe to return to her marked seat with her bag put in place. She removes her bag from her seat, places it beside her on the wooden table, and sits down with a tray of food in her hand and begins gobbling her food one by one, piece by piece, and Dr. Pepper to wash everything down in her digestive system. Elise wipes her brown red soft lips with a cotton napkin, end to end on the sides of her mouth, and lays it down on her food tray. Elise grabs herself up from the wooden chair and table and goes to the nearest trash can to throw away her scraps of food. Elise goes back to her table to grab a hold of her bag and walks toward the doors of the Tampa Campus Center and exits outside of the Tampa Campus Center to wait patiently for her taxicab to arrive soon. Elise pays thirty dollars for her taxicab ride that is fifteen miles from her school when she arrives home. Elise arrives home safely, says a kind good-bye to the taxicab driver, closes the taxicab door near her, and walks up the sidewalk and the steps to her front door, gets her keys out of the bag, and proceeds to unlock the top and lower knobs of the door to enter inside her house. Elise opens the front door of her house, walks into a clean house, closes the front door behind her, lays her bag on the white posh sofa, and goes to the kitchen to grab a cup of water and goes on forth to start her chemistry lab assignments. After Elise completed her chemistry lab assignments, she cooks herself lasagna and then prepares a slice of the lasagna on her plate, and yummy in her tummy! After dinner, Elise heads to her laptop computer to check her e-mail. Elise checks her e-mail on the computer to see if any messages came through on the screen. Quickly, it appears to her attention that she received an e-mail from Lisa's sister, Melissa (the girl Elise met at Tampa State University). Melissa stated in the e-mail a question phrase. The question phrase begins like this: "Hey, Elise, this is Melissa. How are you? I clearly remember us speaking to each other about the Bible group club and you asked me the time, place, and when the following meetings would occur. Well, let me tell you right now what is happening at this time so your question is fully answered." Melissa continues her statement in the e-mail saying, "Elise, to answer your question, the Bible club group is having a meeting next week on Monday. I would like it if you attend. Hope to see you there!"

Then Elise replies back to Melissa's message and says, "Can't wait to see and see what all this is about! Thanks and good-bye!"

Elise checks her other e-mails and then slowly shuts down and closes her laptop computer at the late hour of the night and gets herself ready for bed to begin a fresh new day. In the days of the weekend, Elise does her usual errands along with chores that have to be completed. With errands and chores being done, Elise finds in her spare time to relax during the day with the leisure of watching comedy shows, sitcoms, drama episodes and in-demand movies for TV. Toward the end of the days of Elise's fulfilling weekend, she takes moments to pray to God and dwells in His presence in peace and serenity, thinking about preparing for next week's obligations and responsibilities of school, work, and play (if there is such a thing as play in Elise's frame of mind).

The week has begun. Elise has the usual routine of waking at 7:30 a.m. from her noisy alarm clock to head for the bathroom to first brush her teeth, wash her lovely plain brown face, and take a ten- to fifteen-minute hot shower and then rush to her room to get dressed in a matter of minutes. She then heads for the stairs to grab her backpack and heads out the front door to catch the arrival of her taxicab. At this time, it is Monday—the usual pattern—eat breakfast in the cafeteria, go to classes, and arrive to her home abode. Soon after Monday passed, Friday came.

Friday's were Elise's comfort days where she did not have to attend school and deal with school work. On her Friday's off, Elise would regularly listen to music, play games on the computer, and talk on the phone with her friends (especially those she felt comfortable talking to).

But this particular Friday was not the same predicament like several Fridays before where Elise would just hang around the house doing nothing. On this Friday, Elise seemed a bit bored and wanted to go to school for a different reason. Elise wanted to engage in a productive social group activity. Elise wanted to explore this foreign bible group club at Tampa State University. With a daring and curious mind to venture out and explore, Elise dares to be an adventurer and goes beyond her parent's wishes to schedule a ride to go to school and have an enlightened experience she has not had in her life before. Elise is on the bus on a sunny Friday afternoon as she occasionally browses through the wide windows to see the city streets of Tampa, Florida. While riding, Elise hears a buzz tone on her cell phone. She glances to see who has called her. Elise looks at the number and notices it is her mom calling her. She immediately answers the phone upon pickup.

Elise responses in a quick tone and says, "Hello, oh, oh…hello, Mom."

Mom replies in curious tone, "Hello, how are you?"

"I am good, Mom." Elise quickly thinks about how she will respond. Her voice begins to murmur and breaks apart with a nervous tone. "Hey, Mom…I just want to let you know that I am going to school."

"What are you going for?"

"I am going to school for a meeting."

"What meeting is this?"

"It is a meeting for a Bible club at school, Mom."

"What, why are you telling me this now? How come I have to know about this at the last minute?"

Elise is oblivious to what her mom is saying and purposely ignores what her mom is saying to her and then says in sympathy and remorse, "I am sorry, Mom."

Mom refuses to accept Elise's sympathy and pleading apology and says in a stern tone of voice, "Don't do this again, you hear me, Elise?"

"Yes, Mom."

"Bye."

"Bye."

Elise arrives at Tampa State University, pays her taxi fare, and says good-bye to the driver. She then goes inside the school to find the building to where the club meeting is located. She arrives to the building and enters into another room by an elevator and finds that there are two doors in front of her that are closed with two separate windows to peek in and see what is inside. As Elise is close to the doors with the two windows present in front of her, she peeks through to see what is inside. Inside, she sees a foggy shadow of people standing around in a circle with their heads bent down and holding each other's hands. she waits patiently for a few minutes to see if someone will come out and open the door for her.

In a few minutes, Elise sees a young man with dark skin walk toward her and opens the door. When Elise comes inside, she sees a large room that has many levels of seats in each section and rows. Elise also sees a part of the room that has a long projector white screen, a random table placed in front of the projector screen, and people standing around in a circle holding hands. To shift her focus away from looking at tangible objects, Elise looks toward her view to see the persons standing in front of her. With Elise walking toward what is in front of her, in her mind she is thinking, *Hmm…this is different and unusual to me. Let's see what this is all about.* With each person standing, holding hands, and praying, they notice who is in their presence, but they continue to pray together amongst themselves. Elise smiles and notices her friend Melissa smiling back at her with a "Hello" signal and a hand wave. With everyone around Elise praying, she follows along with what they are doing and closes her eyes to pray with all of them. Then, everyone around along with Elise opens their eyes after they pray. With everyone standing around in a circle with Elise in the "circle group," a young mature man by the name of Robert is present.

Robert looks at Elise in curiosity and says, "What is your name?"

Elise opens up her mouth eagerly with assurance and says, "My name is Elise."

Robert goes on to say with many questions, "Where are you from?"

Elise says in response with looking at Robert's face, "I am from Seattle, Washington."

"Okay, nice to meet you. I am sure everyone here welcomes you too."

Elise is wondering what Robert will say to her next. With everyone in the group staring at Elise intently, Robert springs forth his next question. Robert says, "What happened to you?"

Elise speaks with no hesitation and says in a straight-forward answer, "I have an illness and continue to have an illness."

Everyone in the room sigh with concern and say, "Hmmm…" Robert, hearing Elise's situation, begins to speak with eloquence and says prophetically with joyous announcement, "Are you ready to be healed?"

"Yes, I am."

"Are you ready to receive your healing?"

"I sure am."

Everyone cheers in joyous assemble. Elise is unaware of what is continuing to transpire; she looks around the circle of people and then hears a deep voice coming out of the air and asks her, "How old are you?"

Elise responses to say, "I am twenty-two years old."

The name of this deep voice speaking is Stephan. Stephan looks at Elise in the eyes and says, "How long have you had this illness?"

Elise, intrigued of Stephan's inquisitive nature, says with her eyes looking at him, "I have had this illness since I was born."

Everyone is looking at Stephan and Elise as they have a conversation. After their short conversation, Robert intervenes and asks the group to start praying for Elise's miraculous healing. With Elise's eyes closed, she prays in her heart and spirit, but her ears are not turned off from what she hears. Elise begins to hear the persons amongst her mumbling in many tongues at once which seem weird and strange to her. As they are mumbling in many strange tongues, one young devout and outspoken man begins declaring loudly and prophetically the Word of God, by saying in his words, "Father God, I pray that you would have your way with us, bring your power down, and heal us right now!" Robert keeps on praying these same words repetitively and starts using other prolific words with eloquence and power, but his voice gets louder and louder as he speaks. As Robert's words speed and get louder, the people around him become strangely "eclipsed." The atmosphere in the room begins changing dramatically, but slowly and Elise intuitively attunes what is happening around and transpires in her mind what will happen soon after. Elise figures out what happens next. As Robert continues to pray loudly, Elise hears the people around her start speaking in unknown tongues and hyperventilating dramatically. As the people around her continue to hyperventilate, Elise keeps her eyes closed and prays in her heart. As Elise's eyes are closed, her ears are wide open. Elise could hear people yelling and screaming. With Elise's eyes still closed, she could sense individuals approaching and then they start touching her firmly and speak through her ears. In Elise's ears, voices of people tell her to start moving and walking, but she does not move and can't move. Elise cannot move because she is entangled by members of the Bible club at her every side. At this point, Elise's eyes are still closed. She can't see anything, but her instincts are fully aware of its surroundings. The people in the Bible study club are still in their moments of yelling, screaming, and awkward jollification while Elise is standing still immovable. Elise's eyes continue to remain closed for a long time and she prays in her heart at any moment for this situation that she is in to be over. While Elise wishes the situation would be over, it is not. The people in that large biology room continue to surround themselves around Elise. They continue to touch Elise firmly as they continue to speak in unknown *"bizarre tongues."* With Elise standing still, the people start touching her head, arms, legs, and feet.

With the young people touching every inch of her body, they scream and yell in prayer sounds. Elise starts to be uncomfortable and just decides to keep her eyes closed. As

Elise hears the young people praying in extreme loud tones, some of them start rubbing her legs up and down while others are holding her head, arms, and hands. Elise hears those ahead of her start speaking to her. The voices chant, "Walk, walk, walk!" One peculiar voice out of all the voices Elise hears. That voice strikes her attention and her ears yearn to the voice of Stephan. Elise's eyes are still closed while others are praying loudly for her deliverance. Elise afraid to signal to the voice she hears, she does not move. But Stephan's voice is distinguished among the rest of the voices Elise hears. Stephan says to Elise from the other side of the biology room, "Start moving, start walking." Now when Elise hears Stephan's voice, her ears open up and her eyes begin to slightly open up. Others around her get exuberantly excited and they begin to jump in enthusiasm. With Elise's eyes slightly open, the people that were touching and praying for her released their hands from her. Stephan's voice kept echoing in Elise's ears. Stephan said from a distance, "Walk, keep walking. Don't stop, don't stop! As Elise hears those words with her eyes slightly closed, the voices behind her and Stephan's voice gravitate toward her moving and walking in the center of the large biology room.